For Sam and Kate and
the cosy, cosy nights ~ A. H.

To D. A. R. and K. G. J. (because big boys
have to take their medicine too) ~ A. J.

Don't You Feel Well, Sam?

Amy Hest illustrated by Anita Jeram

First published 2002 by Walker Books Ltd
87 Vauxhall Walk, London SE11 5HJ

This edition published 2003

2 4 6 8 10 9 7 5 3

Text © 2002 Amy Hest Illustrations © 2002 Anita Jeram

The right of Amy Hest and Anita Jeram to be identified as author and illustrator respectively of this
work has been asserted by them in accordance with the Copyright, Designs and Patents Act 1988

This book has been typeset in Contemporary Brush Bold

Printed in China

British Library Cataloguing in Publication Data:
a catalogue record for this book is available from the British Library

ISBN 0-7445-9839-7

www.walkerbooks.co.uk

WALKER BOOKS
AND SUBSIDIARIES
LONDON · BOSTON · SYDNEY · AUCKLAND

It was a cold, cold night
on Plum Street.

In the little white house,
Mrs Bear was putting Sam to bed.
She closed their favourite book and
they both blew out the candle.
"Kiss good night, Sam," Mrs Bear said.
And she wrapped him all cosy
in the blanket that was red.

But suddenly she heard a cough – *Hck, hck!*
And there sat Sam, curled up
and small and coughing
in his bed.

Mrs Bear put her arms round Sam.
"Don't you feel well, Sam?"
Sam shook his head. *Hck, hck!*
"Poor Sam." Mrs Bear hugged
him harder and kissed his warm cheek.
"You have a cough," she said.

And she dashed down
the stairs — and up
again — with syrup.

"Open wide, Sam!" Mrs Bear said.
Sam shook his head. "Tastes *bad*," he said.
"Yes," said his mama. "You need to be brave."
Sam put the blanket on his head.

"I *don't* have a cough!" *Hck, hck!*

"Try again, Sam," said his mama.
Sam shook the blanket off his head.
He opened up, then closed his
mouth tight. The spoon was too big.

"Too big," said Sam.
Hck, hck!

"You can do it," Mrs Bear said.
"I *know* you can, Sam!"
Sam opened up, then
closed his mouth tight.
Too much syrup
on a too-big spoon.

"Too much," said Sam.
Hck, hck!

Mrs Bear rubbed frost off the window and peeped outside. "Soon it will snow," she said.

"Open wide, Sam, and afterwards we'll go downstairs and wait for snow."

Snow!

Sam opened wide.
Then very wide.
He spluttered and snorted
and made a big face
and the syrup went down.

"Brave Sam,"
he said.

Mrs Bear and Sam
held hands on the stairs.
Sam wore his dressing-
gown that was blue and
his slippers were, too.

They lit a little fire in the kitchen,
then made a pot of tea.
Mrs Bear put extra honey
in the tea and it was
nice sliding down.

After tea, they sat in the big purple chair
near the window and waited for snow.
Mrs Bear told a story about a bear
called Sam. Sam liked the story,
so she told it again.

Hck, hck! went the cough,
every now and then.

Sam leaned back on his mama's soft tummy, and it wriggled while she talked. The little fire glowed and the kitchen was warm.

All through the night, Mrs Bear and Sam sat in the big purple chair and waited.

And finally
it snowed.